CW01080573

ZEMINRA

*The Mission To Find The
Enchanted Steel*

Tafseer Zainab

TZ studios

Thank you to my family who supported me. Also to my siblings who motivated and annoyed me while writing this book
Stay creative and be happy!!!! :)

" Girls can do anything that Boys can do, if not better"

PROLOGUE

In a land far ,far away, there is a place called Zeminra...

And there is a war

There is a war between Elves and Reglins.

Zeminra is divided into three parts.

Elves,Goblins and Reglins.Elves and Goblins are kind and creative.Reglins like to destroy.The three formed a treaty between them but Reglins kept on breaking them.

They gave Elves a hard time.

Elves were reluctant but both Reglins and Elves agreed that they would both have a battle between them .They had 2 months to prepare.

The one who lost would have to move away or perish.

However, the Elves had another problem.If not fixed, would turn them into unfair,unjust,cruel people

ZEMINRA

The Mission To Find The Enchanted Steel

CHAPTER 1

"**E**lves of Zeminra! If we want our children to grow and evolve, we must find the rare metal steel to protect our brave courageous soldiers and have less martyrs," the old weak leader said in a desperate voice. "But who will be our saviour? Step forward our chosen one. We need you to defeat the cruel, bloodthirsty Reglins."

A long awkward silence came...There were nervous hushed whispers spreading around the room. Tap. Tap. Hundreds of eyes shifted to a small corner in the room. A small, short girl stepped forward confidently. Her cheeks blushed a pale red as she realised the amount of attention she was getting.

"I'll go," the girl said in a soft deep voice.

She was Megadelina. The brave girl was a mix of Goblin and Elf, two very parallel species. She had the beauty of an Elf and the strength and toughness of a Goblin. She wore jewel-embedded earrings that dangled from her eyes. They made soft tinkle sounds when she walked and ran. She was about 50 centimetres tall, which is tall for an elf. However, Megadelina was also a mix of Goblin and Elf, so this was a normal height for her. Her hair pours down and is shinier than marble and silkier than silk. She didn't talk much with her neighbours but said hi every now and then. Megadelina carried a pretty satchel that had embroidery of leaves and flowers. There was a big M in the middle, standing for her name. She self-taught herself to embroidery and paint and loved doing it as her hobby and passion. She was 13 years old and all her classmates at Zeminra Elf school assumed she was timid and feeble. However, their minds would change very soon....

Her freckles glowed slightly, nervously waiting for the leader to respond back. There was a painful silence as the people tried to absorb what just happened. Their faces were blank as if they didn't know how to respond. Suddenly, the room blasted with laughter! Fingers pointed aggressively at Megadelina as she stood there confidently. As the laughter grew louder and louder Megadelina tried to rewind back to try and figure out what she stated that was so funny.

A couple of moments later (or what felt like a million years) the crowd slightly calmed down so they could hear what the leader was saying. "You! You! You will fulfil the quest?" the leader said, joining with the crazy chaotic dim -minded crowd. They mocked and laughed and annoyed and teased until the whole room was full of overwhelming noise that bounced of the cold metal walls as mocking echoes.

Megadelina's freckles started glowing dark red and the pointy bit of her hat started to fold imitating a frown. A really cross frown." I will show you how brave I am! Just you wait and see!" Megadelina yelled over the hectic room. Just a bunch of stupid hyenas, Megadelina thought. When the crowd was busy laughing, Megadelina sprinted to nearby table and leapt onto it, expertly snatching a piece of paper that was in the leader 's giant fat, plump hand. "Hey-"the leader began to say.

"Whether you like it or not. I Megadelina will find the enchanted steel and save all of us," Megadelina announced. Normally, she would have stage fright when making a speech like this. However, this was serious and Megadelina didn't care at the moment. Before the others could do anything, Megadelina hurried to her apartment (yes, she was 13 and had her own apartment). Her pointed ears wiggled excitedly as she looked out of her diamond shaped window, deeply thinking about the long journey ahead of her. Megadelina was filled with so many emotions and a billion thoughts that she thought she would get sick. They tugged at her and made her doubtful and anxious. The laughs of the people stuck in her head as she tried to get rid of them. She shook her head. No. They are wrong! I can and will do this and will not give up!

The sky was blending into a warm brown, like the sky was filled with sweet, delicious hot chocolate. The sun's green rays pierced through the joyful yellow clouds. Megadelina soon fell asleep.

CHAPTER 2

The next morning Megadelina woke up and walked to her kitchen to feed her beloved pet Zemidork, whose fuzzy tail waved excitedly. Megadelina didn't talk much to other people (she tried to, but people just thought she was strange and weird), so she talked a lot to Zemidork. Zemidork was a lovely furry creature. She was a type of cat with only one eye. Zemidork has always followed her owner everywhere but was too tired to come and follow Megadelina to the meeting last night. Zemidork may be a mystical creature, but she still has the lazy characteristics of normal cats.

"Zemidork my dear friend, we have a great adventure ahead of us," Megadelina told Zemidork, standing majestically with pride. The unusual thing about Megadelina's village was that they lived in a huge bunker with tunnels and secret passageways instead of a traditional hut or cottage. The Village did this so that they could protect themselves from the wicked Reglins. Megadelina had lots of reasons to hate and like the bunker. One thing she hated about the bunker was that the walls were cold and lifeless. The good thing was that it was a fun place because of its secret tunnels and passageways. She loved roaming about and discovering new tunnels where she could read and write and draw. Recently she made a little fort in a small room that was never used by anyone. She carefully decorated and painted the walls with emerald-green leaves and eyepopping sketches of flowers and trees. She added candles that smelt of delicate roses which could calm down even the most stressed. The bunker was built after a few years since Megadelina was born so she did experience some of her toddlerhood in a traditional hit or cottage. However, those memories were very vague and faint. Megadelina sometimes daydreamed about her life in a cottage, full of wildlife and a peaceful garden right beside her. She grinned, excited to see what her journey ahead would be like.

Megadelina walked out of her apartment and then climbed the ladder that leaded her out of the bunker. Zemidork trotted behind. Megadelina peered out of the highest hole in the hill. Zemidork gradually catches. Zemidork was more of a nocturnal animal. up. Megadelina needed to go to the Chanen forest according to the map. However, the Chanen forest was known to be full of tremendous monsters that were lurking there. Megadelina did not believe those myths. She thought that forest were amazing sights with beautiful woodland creatures and multicoloured birds tweeting to their hearts content. Creeping cautiously towards that direction of the Chanen forest, Megadelina tried to push away her anxious thoughts that kept on irritatingly popping up in her overthinking mind. It was as hard as getting rid of cockroaches! Or even gum stuck in your hair!

Zemidork being with her owner for more than 5 years understood everything. Her reddish-brown fur turned puffier and fluffier and soon she looked like an overweight pufferfish. This peculiar act that Zemidork did meant that she was feeling horrific fear.

Laying her first few footsteps onto the musty grown of the deep and endless Chanen forest, Megadelina felt chills on her spine. Her legs were so shaky that she felt like she would collapse any second. Megadelina glanced at what was ahead of her. Her dreams of an idyllic forest got crushed. Pitch black. Total darkness. She could see nothing that was ahead of her. What was she going to do? While she was thinking, Zemidork started walking towards the forest with ease. That's it! Megadelina thought. Zemidork could lead them. Why? Well, that is because Zemidork is a cat and since she is a mystical creature her night vision is enhanced twice because instead of it being shared in two eyes it is all concentrated into her one eye! Megadelina's face shone bright, her eyes glittering, and all her worries washed away. She found new unstoppable confidence.

CHAPTER 3

After hours of walking in blind eyes, Megadelina sat down near a tree and drank water that she kept in her satchel. She prepared this bag with all the equipment and supplies she might need: a few apples, water, the map, a rope, matches, sleeping bag and a pocketknife. She loved apples since they were so convenient. You could toss it the waste away knowing that the apple would rot and biograde into a great fertilizer for the plants nearby. It is kind of like giving charity to nature! (don't start throwing apples on the street though. Always throw it in the bin) She sat there enjoying the tranquillity of the forest. Megadelina was exhausted from walking for miles and miles. When would this forest ever end? She yawned as she gazed at whatever was in front of her. The forest was still very dark. Sssssss! Megadelina flinched. What was that? Megadelina's heart beat fast. Sssssssss! Megadelina looked above. Her heart dropped a beat.

Up there in the tree was wickedly grinning, an anaconda. It slid smoothly down the truck of the tree deciding whether to squeeze Megadelina to her death or not. Since Megadelina was a mix of goblin and elf, she was smaller than a human (about 50 cm tall the last time she checked) so she was a great snack for the vile beast. Megadelina stayed calm (or at least tried to). She had to think quickly. In her school, there was one programme called the Art of Survival where they learned how to fight dangerous creatures. However, she didn't want to hurt the beast. She would only hurt the beast as a last resort. She knew that anacondas were not venomous so the beast wouldn't bite. Surprisingly, instead of not trapping Megadelina, the anaconda tried to strangle Zemidork who Megadelina swiftly picked up and ran. The anaconda in return snarled at Megadelina, staring at her with raging yellow eyes as its prey was safely in the enemy's arms.

CHAPTER 4

Sprinting, Megadelina ran and ran. She didn't care if her legs were suffering from scratches and bruises from thorns and nettles. Her arms ached from holding Zemidork, but Megadelina didn't care. She was relieved that she was able to save- Thud. "Wow!!" Megadelina yelled. She bumped into a tree. She was so focused in running away that she forgot she couldn't see in such a dark pitch-black place. "You are so smart Megadelina," Megadelina muttered to herself. She slapped her forehead in regret. She patted her clouds to get rid of the dust and moved on.

This time Megadelina made sure she was following Zemidork the whole time. Megadelina's eyes widened as she gazed carefully at what was ahead of her. There was a bright light at the end of the forest. The sudden bright light nearly blinded Megadelina for real. Megadelina got perplexed. This wasn't in the map! With no warnings a storm arrived and there were huge sounds of thunder roaring at the forest. Wow! That was unexpected, Megadelina thought with concern. The light dimmed and she saw two red glowing circles in the distance. Assuming they were fire torches Megadelina decided to go forward...Did she make the right choice?

CHAPTER 5

As Megadelina tentatively walked towards the two red circles Megadelina realised she just made a mistake. She gasped in horror. Was this reality? Megadelina sighed. She was too exhausted for another tragedy. The two fiery circles weren't fire torches! The circles were eyes that were filled with glowing red blood that was filled with pure hatred and malice. Its breath smelt like the stink of 1,000 rotten eggs concentrated into a small juice box that you get in multipacks that are only 255ml big. Megadelina pinched her nose in disgust and tried not vomit. Who was this awful, stinky beast? What should she do now? The anaconda a few hours ago was a mere fly compared to this appalling beast. Megadelina stumbled and fell. Why did she have to trip right now?

Megadelina's eyes grew wide with terror. Her legs and arms had frozen. She felt petrified. Megadelina panicked as she couldn't move her body at all. She was paralyzed and helpless. It seemed like stench of the beast had completely taken over her mind.

"I must be calm. I need to be calm," Megadelina tried to assure herself even though it would be useless. I need a heavy rock, Megadelina thought. "Zemidork! Fetch that rock!"

Zemidork nimbly pounced towards the monster and without any effort, dodged the long sticky tongue that the monster kept thrashing on the ground. It had strange scales all around its sapphire blue spiky tail. The beast had 10 tails that banged on the ground, making cracks and earthquakes where Zemidork could fall into. However, Zemidork was very agile and athletic and could dodge all the ten noxious tails and obstacles with mastery. Zemidork whizzed to Megadelina in a speed that was quicker than light and gave the rock to her. Megadelina observed the rock carefully, noting its features. It was a heavy, dense rock weighing 2.5 kg and had spikey sharp bits that could tear at flesh easily. Megadelina positioned her arm in a throwing pose, the scaly tale of the beast appeared from the back of its head and wrapped around her arm. Megadelina felt the weird slimy monster's tail and every single scale that it had. Megadelina held her breath as the poor girl thought of all the possible ways this could go wrong. She felt so helpless and paralysed. Her body went limp, and she could finally feel all the aches and sores that she had on her legs and arms.

Megadelina felt sick. Suddenly, the tail shook her arm so violently that Megadelina felt like her arm was about to fall out any second. She closed her eyes and cried in agony. Her arm throbbed so bad that she thought her arm was ripping into a million pieces. The pain was so atrocious that she hoped that the monster would gulp her so that the pain would stop. She couldn't take up enough courage to open her eyes as she imagined that what she saw wouldn't be so pretty. "Zemidork, help me!!", shrieked Megadelina to her. Megadelina didn't know how or what her pet would do but at least she had warned her. Megadelina gripped the rock as hard as she could but now that she saw that there would be no point Megadelina dropped it with disappointment. The beast then stopped shaking her arm so aggressively. Megadelina looked at the creature with shock. The beast was quite clever. Instead of risking getting hit by a possible weapon it first disarmed its prey.

The tired but amused girl examined the monster carefully. The monster waited patiently (which is exceedingly rare for monsters) Scanning all the weird, unusual features on its face, Megadelina finally determined the species of the beast. The beast obviously was some type of a humungous reptile since it had peculiar scales and spikes on its skin. The monster opened its mouth and showed Megadelina all its nooks and crannies as it was at the dentist showing her its rotting teeth and cavities that smelt so putrid and rancid that a sensitive person could faint at the slight sniff of it. "You really need to brush your teeth," suggested Megadelina. The beast just growled at her. In its huge jaw were long pointy fangs that dripped with glooming purple acid ominously. It's razor -sharp teeth were so sharp-edged that it could tear any fleshful animal into one bite unlike normal creatures. Of course, the monster was obviously fed up with the constant staring that Megadelina was doing (like anyone would be) so decided to make irritating slurping sounds that disturbed Megadelina's thinking (does that remind you of your annoying sibling)

You are a Chingle aren't you?" Megadelina assumed, hoping it wasn't.

The monster grinned evilly and nodded. Chingles aren't the type of beasts that you want to meet in your everyday park stroll. They are quite rare in forest like environments and prefer to live in colder habitats such as mountains. More specifically, in caves. Chingles are quite giant, being huger than elephants. Something clicked into Megadelina's mind. Chingles were not lizards.! Something was wrong. Megadelina turned impatient. She felt angry at herself. Why could she not figure out what she was looking for? Caves...Fangs...Scales....eyes that were blood red... "That's it! You are a dragon!" Megadelina said, proud of her investigation. The dragon breathed fire to celebrate. The monster was happy that someone had finally recognised its true identity in 1,000 years.

It sneered and shadowed her as she tried to

scurry away. The strange beast opened its mouth and slowly approached Megadelina with hatred in its eyes. Megadelina was terrified with shock. She glanced around to find Zemidork who was hiding in a nearby bush, shivering. Megadelina gave a signal for her to run but Zemidork ran to her owner to get one last cuddle Megadelina told Zemidork to run away but she wouldn't budge "Go!" Megadelina commanded to Zemidork, but she still wouldn't move. Her heart grew warm, and she smiled at her loyal pet. At least she wasn't alone. Her spine chilled as she looked at the gross fangs of the monster. Disgusting.

Megadelina closed her eyes in fear and disgust (mostly disgust) She just wanted the monster to gulp her in one try and get over with it. One...two...three...Megadelina counted to 50 but nothing happened. What? Slowly opening her eyes, Megadelina hoped she wasn't in a river full of stomach acid. That would be nasty. "Please be alive, please be alive," chanted Megadelina, hoping that by chanting her wish would be granted. She was outraged as she saw the Chingle holding clenching the map between its jaws.

"No! Not the map!" Megadelina cried, chasing the monster. Luckily, Megadelina was half Elf and half Goblin. Therefore, she had strong legs that she could almost 30 mile per hour, which is way faster than some elite athletes could ever manage. This meant that she could chase the monster easily. The problem was that the beast had jumped over from a huge cliff to another cliff that was across. The gap was at least 3 metres long. Just a reminder that Megadelina was only 50 cm tall and the monster 2 meters long. Plus the monster had powerful strong legs that it could pounce far away with. Megadelina was disappointed as she realised the consequences. While the monster ran away in the distance, a strange white animal swooped down and followed the Chingle. It was as if it was chasing the huge beast. However, Megadelina took no notice of that. She had destroyed the opportunity to save Zeminra and show the people that she was capable of more than they thought. Maybe they were right. Maybe she really had no potential to be the saviour of Zeminra. She was foolish to think that she was able to complete the mission. Her fists shook aggressively.

Megadelina sat near a log and wept. One thing that Megadelina needed to work on was that she gave up too quickly. Even though she was super athletic and agile, what was the point in having all that if she was too quick to give up and was impatient? Zemidork saw the sadness of her owner and carved something on the dusty ground. She patted Megadelina with her soft delicate paw and showed sympathy to her. Megadelina looked up and smiled at Zemidork gratefully. "What would I do without you?" Megadelina, said in a quiet voice, her eyes pleading for a miracle. Zemidork presented to

Megadelina what she had made.

It said: Crying won't solve your problems. You need to act to make things right.

At the end of the message there was a little heart to show how much she loved her owner. Zemidork meowed at Megadelina, hoping that her little message would help. Megadelina found self-esteem in the message and said, "You're right." Her voice sounded stable and Zemidork understood that the little spell had worked. You just had to believe it to make it work. Megadelina wiped her tears and started thinking. Maybe if she attached her rope to a heavy rock or branch, she could throw it to the other side and then monkey climb all over to the other side. Megadelina got to work straight away and started scavenging for a suitable rock or branch.

After a few hours Megadelina found a great branch that was durable and 10kg heavy. Now she just had to find a way to efficiently throw the branch faraway without risking breaking her arm. While she scanned the other cliff, she blocked all her senses so that she could only focus on the cliff's features. No luck. Megadelina roared and threw the branch away in frustration. This was not going to be easy.

"Megadelina," a mysterious woman's voice spoke.

Megadelina turned around in utter shock. Megadelina opened her mouth to speak but nothing came out. Her mouth was stuck in a gaping mouth kind of face...Who was this person?...

CHAPTER 6

After the effects of shock, Megadelina's mouth paralysis finally wore off and Megadelina asked "Who are you?". Megadelina felt a strange sense of familiarity. As if she had met this person before. Megadelina brushed away this thought off. She couldn't trust this woman right away

There were jewel embedded clips that were placed on the black hair of her. The hair was so black and smooth that it looked like a black waterfall was gushing behind her head. The hair went up to the lady's waist and Megadelina looked at it with awe. Even Zemidork's one eye widened by only giving one glance at her. Zemidork let the lady pet her. "You have a beautiful cat," the lady complimented.

"You didn't answer my question," Megadelina reminded politely. Megadelina was grateful for the compliment, but Zemidork's and her safety came first. They had no idea who this lady was, and she could be dangerous. The woman wore a white robe that was gold at the edges. It was a slim dress and was so long that it nearly touched the ground.in her right hand she had a long gold staff that was decorated with Sapphires and Emeralds and Opals with a weird white Crystal in the middle of the stick.

The woman finally answered. "I am Queen Megadeline. The queen of your village," the Queen answered, shaking hands with Megadelina. "You have been a brave elf. So, for your reward I will give you the enchanted Steel," the proud Queen gave Megadelina the steel as the surprised girl looked at it with satisfaction. (Queen Megadeline's name ends with an "e" instead of an "a")

Zeminra was saved! But what would they do with such a small piece of steel? "Don't worry I have a huge bucket full of these that you can use." Queen Megadeline replied. Did she just read my mind? Megadelina thought.

"No of course not! I can see your feelings on your face. You are as easy to read as a book," Queen Megadeline corrected. Megadelina flinched. I am going to start practicing controlling my expressions, Megadelina thought.

"With expressions like yours, you could be a great actor. Maybe even win an Oscar award in your first film!" the Queen spoke chuckling loudly. Megadelina blushed as the queen laughed and laughed. I wonder if I could be a great comedian. People seem to laugh at every word I say, Megadelina thought remembering of the time when the whole meeting room started laughing and mocking. Megadelina shuddered at the memory of it. She looked for Zemidork to get comfort, but the cat was watching the Queen intently.

After the lady stopped laughing, she invited Megadelina to ride on her magic carpet that she made appear out of thin air. The carpet was intricate and had lots of beautiful bright colours and designs that looked like it took forever to make. In the middle of the carpet there was a huge M which was probably were the initials of the Queen's name. Megadelina feeling fatigued, joyfully said yes. She never had sat on a magical carpet so was very content to ride it.

After flying a few hours, the Queen finally decided to tell the true identity of her.

"I am your mother Megadelina. Your father is the king of the Goblins. I chose to move to his kingdom because I couldn't bear to see how this village was turning into a patriarchal society. Patriarchal society means a place where boys rule over girls. They underestimated us young girls. I was too coward to fix this place, so I left this village. I don't know if I can ever forgive myself. Would...Would you forgive me?" Queen Megadeline said, sounding as if she was going to burst into tears at any moment.

"I forgive you. Just make sure that you learn from

your mistakes and don't repeat them," Megadelina advised, smiling at Queen Megadeline. "Oh! Also, never give up!" The Queen smiled back with appreciation.

CHAPTER 7

As they glide through cheerful crowds the people applauded and encouraged them with whistles and hurrahs. Megadelina smiled as her classmates were staring at the Queen and her with awe. Their eyes were wide and glittering with curiosity. When Megadelina got off the carpet they started asking her a thousand questions. It was like they would never run out. "Okay. Okay. I Will answer them all right. Be patient!" Megadelina told their eager faces. Be patient. That was one thing that she had learned, to be patient.

Queen Megadeline got confused since she only saw a plain grass hill in front of her. "Where do you live?"

Megadelina politely showed her the way to the meeting where everybody started shouting again with joy. The happy cheers turned into annoying echoes as the cold metal walls echoed the sounds into awful deafening noises. Queen Megadeline put her hand up and the crowd silenced at once. Queen Megadeline was not used to these echoes. The Elves looked in astonishment. They were also hypnotised with her beauty. "After the war with the Reglins we need to build a better community with cottages and huts. Not this metal prison that you have been forced to be live in all these years in," The Queen announced in a sweet but serious tone. There were hushed whispers as the people agreed with the Queen.

Tap. Tap. The people looked above as they heard heavy boots smacking the heavy metal ceiling. The leader had arrived. He was surprised to hear so much commotion and clamour. His jaw dropped as he looked up to see Queen Megadeline. His face turned into shock to happiness as he invited the Queen to rule their village and help conduct their army. The Queen accepted this with no second thought. The leader asked why she had left, and the Queen explained her reason. The people looked at themselves with shame and guilt. They each said sorry one by one. Megadelina felt sympathy for the people as they started looking so sad and ashamed. "It's okay. You don't have to sulk about this forever. Just promise that you will never underestimate anyone ever again," Megadelina said beaming.

"Shall we have a party?" Queen Megadelina asked. The room blew up with screams and yells. Queen Megadeline covered her ears. Her face looked irritated, and she gave Megadelina -not again! - look.

Megadelina giggled. She still couldn't believe that such an interesting woman was her mother.

CHAPTER 8

The next day, people set up their shops and workshops where they set up their interesting paintings, woodworks, sculptures and so much more. There was even a horse-riding and archery workshop! People wore their best clothes and sang and danced to their heart's content. Even woodland birds came to tweet along with them. Queen Megadeline used her magic to make pretty idyllic flowers that stood up with pride and boasted about their delicate petals. Megadelina played with her classmates and made friends that she had never made before. They played hide and seek and joined Megadelina to paint in one of the workshops. She Soon heavy rain starts, and children started screaming and laughing. Even the adults become silly. The shop owners? Yeah....they weren't too happy about the rain. Oh! Zemidork? You could say that the rain and her were mortal enemies for an awfully long time. She may be a mystical creature with only one eye, but she still was a cat after all!

EPILOGUE

Soon the village started to build their huts and cottages and their life turned peaceful again.Thanks to Megadelina and the Queen's amazing experience ,she had won the war successfully and the Elves cheered as this was an important deal for them.

They had also fixed their mindset of underestimating girls and now they are treated the same as boys.

The story of Megadelina's journey to find the Enchanted Steel was told again and again in generations and generations of Elves to come.They painted beautiful drawings and tried to be creative and kind.

The End

Thank you for reading this book,

If you liked this story ,it would be helpful if you wrote a review on Amazon and recommended this book to your family and freinds.It was a lot of fun writing this book and I enjoyed the process

STAY CREATIVE AND BE HAPPY !!! :)

ABOUT THE AUTHOR

Tafseer Zainab

I am a teen author and I love writing stories :)
Writing stories is cool...

Be a writer....Its fun

Printed in Great Britain
by Amazon

81546016R00031